Belly Laughs From Bikini Bottom

Stephen Hillenberg

Based on the TV series *SpongeBob SquarePants*® created
by Stephen Hillenberg as seen on Nickelodeon®

SIMON SPOTLIGHT
An imprint of Simon & Schuster Children's Publishing Division
1230 Avenue of the Americas, New York, New York 10020
Copyright © 2003 Viacom International Inc. All rights reserved.
NICKELODEON, *SpongeBob SquarePants*, and all related titles, logos, and characters are
trademarks of Viacom International Inc.
All rights reserved, including the right of reproduction in whole or in part in any form.
SIMON SPOTLIGHT and colophon are registered trademarks
of Simon & Schuster.
Manufactured in the United States of America
6 8 10 9 7 5
ISBN-13: 978-0-689-86165-9
ISBN-10: 0-689-86165-6
1210 OFF

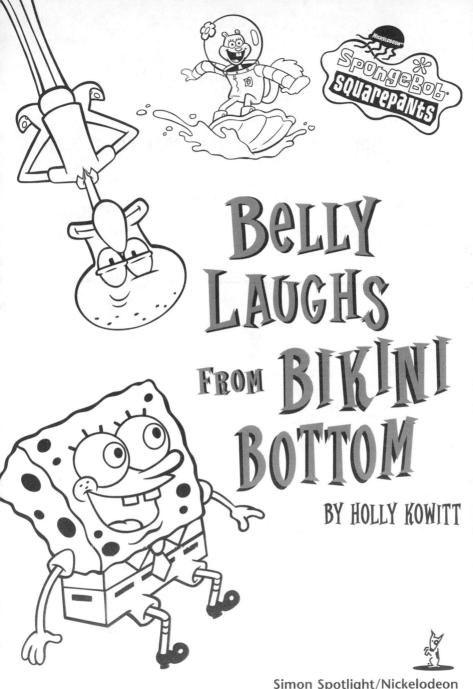

BELLY LAUGHS

FROM BIKINI BOTTOM

BY HOLLY KOWITT

Simon Spotlight/Nickelodeon

New York   London   Toronto   Sydney   Singapore

For He's a Jolly Good Yellow:

SpongeBob's Favorite Jokes About Himself

What is SpongeBob's
Favorite place in
New York City?

Times Square.

Why did
SpongeBob buy
a new karate outfit?

It was on his
chopping list.

Why is it easy to trap SpongeBob?

Because he's always cornered.

Why did SpongeBob pay for dinner?

He doesn't like to sponge off his friends.

Did you know?

Sponges absorb the equivalent of sixty-four glasses of water a day!

What is SpongeBob's
favorite party game?

Truth or Square.

Where does
SpongeBob
go when he
makes a
mistake?

Back to
square one.

How do you measure
SpongeBob?

In square feet.

Did you know?

Small sponges can be less than
one inch long. Large sponges
can be up to six feet long!

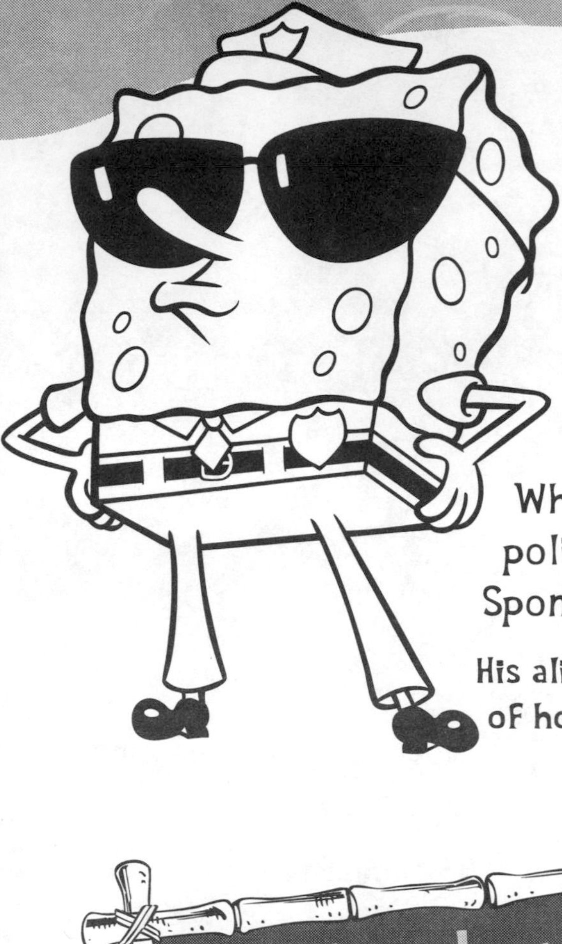

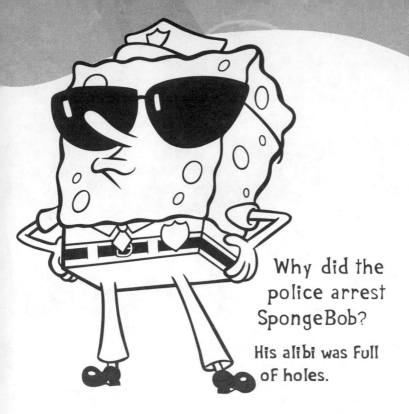

Why did the police arrest SpongeBob?

His alibi was full of holes.

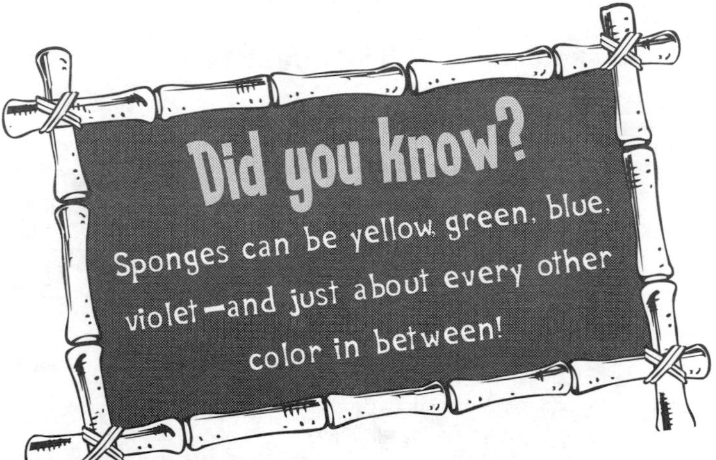
Did you know?
Sponges can be yellow, green, blue, violet—and just about every other color in between!

Why did SpongeBob wear two shirts to play golf?

In case he got a hole in one.

Why did SpongeBob put a clock on the stove?

He wanted to see time Fry.

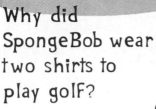

SPONGEBOB'S BOOKSHELF

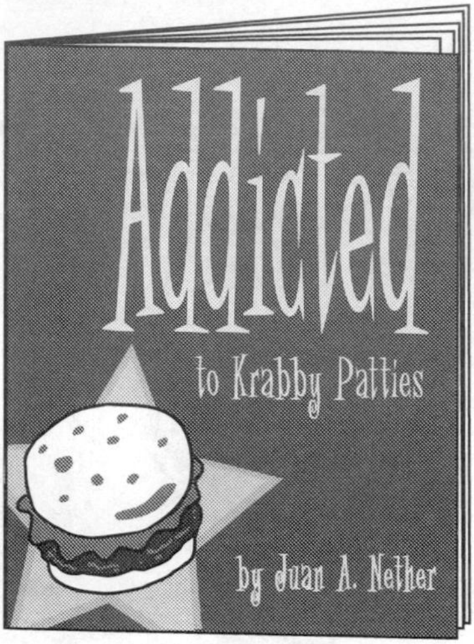
Addicted
to Krabby Patties
by Juan A. Nether

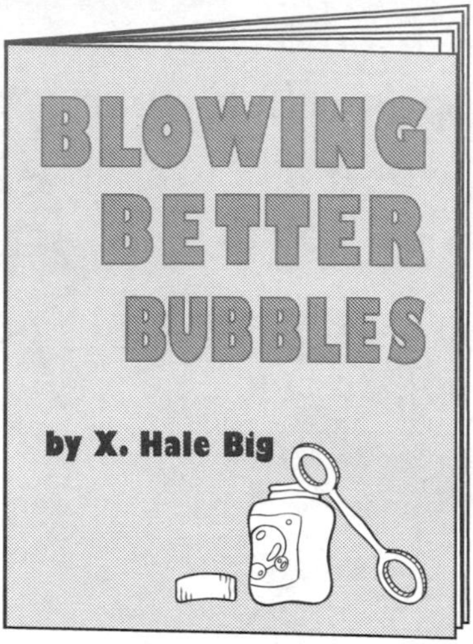
BLOWING
BETTER
BUBBLES
by X. Hale Big

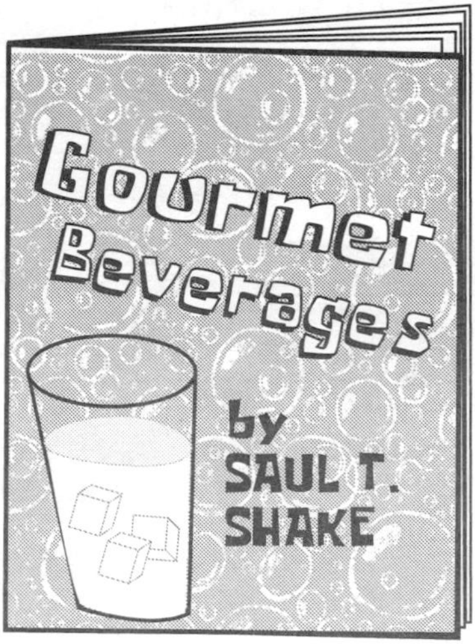
Gourmet
Beverages
by
SAUL T.
SHAKE

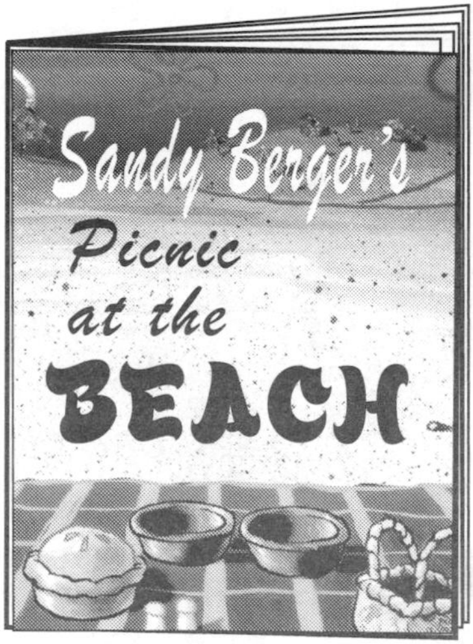
Sandy Berger's
Picnic
at the
BEACH

The Story of Patrick and SpongeBob
by Bess Budz

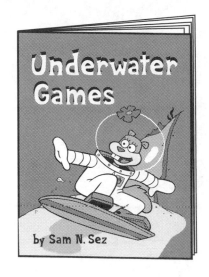

Underwater Games
by Sam N. Sez

Where to Sit in Class
by Wayne Front

PLEASED TO EAT YOU!
BY BARRY KUDA

My Snail Ate My Homework

Why did Mrs. Puff throw her exam in the ocean?

She wanted to test the waters.

Where does Mrs. Puff send sick boating students?

To see the dock.

Why did Mrs. Puff bring birdseed to school?

She had a parrot-teacher conference.

What did the reef like about school?

Giving coral reports.

School Blues

What is the best way
for SpongeBob
to learn?

**Let it all
soak in.**

How did the whale feel when
she got suspended?

A little blue.

How's Boating School?

Plankton: I'm at the bottom of my class.

Swordfish: I often cut school.

Algae: We cover a lot of subjects.

Did you know?

The blue whale is the largest animal ever to live on Earth. The record length for a blue whale is 110 feet—that's as big as three school buses lined up!

Eat, Drink and Be Gary!

How does Gary get to the beach?
He takes the shell-evator.

Why did Gary
go to
Hollywood?

To be in slow
business.

How do you clean Gary?

With snail polish.

What did Gary say
when he hurt himself?

Me-OW!

Did you know?

A garden snail travels at
.03 miles per hour.

Just Squidding

Where does Squidward
sleep when he camps?

Z-Z-Z

In a tentacle.

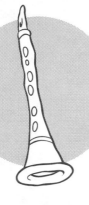

What is Squidward's
Favorite girl's name?

Clara Nett

Did you know?

Tentacles are covered with
powerful suction cups.

How is Squidward like a tennis instructor?

They both know how to raise a racket.

Squidward: What's the best day for a Krabby Patty?

SpongeBob: Fry day!

She's Nutty!

How is SpongeBob's
favorite squirrel
like the beach?

Both are Sandy

What does
SpongeBob say
to cheer on Sandy?

"You go, squirrel!"

What does Sandy
read in school?

Tex books.

What's Sandy's Favorite ballet?

The Nutcracker.

A Whale of a Girl

Why did Pearl slap
the river?

Because it was freshwater.

How does Pearl
like her steak
cooked?

Whale done.

Why does Pearl like the ocean?

She's buoy crazy!

What did one whale say to the other whale?

"Say it, don't spray it!"

What's Pearl's favorite country?

Wales.

Did you know?
The United Kingdom consists of England, Wales, and Scotland.

Baby, I'm a Star(fish)!

Why did Patrick put on another jacket while he was painting?

The can said to add two coats.

SpongeBob: What do you call bubbles who are close pals?

Patrick: Best suds.

What do you get when you cross
Patrick with a cowboy?

A shooting star.

Why did Patrick bury his boom box?

Because the batteries were dead!

Why did Patrick carry a baseball mitt?

He wanted to catch a wave.

How did Patrick find his report card on the ocean's bottom?

He was **deep C fishing.**

REPORT CARD

ENGLISH
BOATING
MATH

Why did Patrick get running shoes?

To be a track star.

Did you know?

Starfish are also called sea stars because they are not really a kind of fish.

Plankton Teasers

Why did the mermaid
turn down a date
with Plankton?

She was **going out
with the tide.**

How do you make
a chocolate
plankton shake?

**Give him a
chocolate bar
and take him to a
scary movie.**

What did the train
conductor say
when he saw
Plankton?

"Small aboard!"

Fill in the Plank-ton:

(Hint: The opposite of tall)

WHAT IS PLANKTON'S ...

Favorite Food?:
strawberry _ _ _ _ _ cake

baseball position?:
_ _ _ _ _ stop

dream job?:
_ _ _ _ _ -order cook

Favorite thing to read?:
_ _ _ _ _ stories

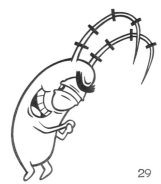

Krabs Jabs

Why did Mr. Krabs put a clock under the counter?

He wanted SpongeBob to work overtime.

What does Mr. Krabs look for on the beach?

Sand dollars.

Why did Mr. Krabs go outside?

He was hoping for some change in the weather.

Why does Mr. Krabs like pelicans?

They always have big bills.

How do you punish Mr. Krabs?

Give him a dime-out.

Where is Mr. Krabs's favorite place?

His living quarters.

Krusty Krab Gags

Why did the
Krabby Patty
go to the gym?

It wanted better buns.

How can you tell Krabby Patties come
from the bottom of the ocean?

They're deep-fried.

Patrick: What do
you give someone
who turns a
year older?

SpongeBob:
A birthday patty!

Mr. Krabs: What do you tell the ocean when it comes to The Krusty Krab?

SpongeBob: It's a pleasure to surf you.

Just Beachy

What do you serve at an underwater brunch?

Drench toast.

Who's listed at the underwater FBI?

America's Moist Wanted.

Where do guest
seashells sleep?

On the Foldout conch.

Patrick: Why did the tide go out?

SpongeBob: It got a Foam call.

What do you bring
to the ocean's
birthday party?

Water balloons.

Why was the ocean embarrassed?

Everyone could see its bottom.

What do people think at the bottom of the ocean?

Deep thoughts.

Who plays the best music on the beach?

Fiddler crabs.

What's a sea monster's favorite meal?

Fish 'n' ships.

Keeping It Reel

Why did the jellyfish join Squidward's band?

To be the lead stinger.

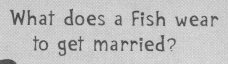

What does a fish wear to get married?

A wetting dress.

What do Fish take to stay healthy?

Vitamin sea.

Did you know?

JellyFish are hatched From eggs.

What do rich
lobsters wear?

Designer claws.

What do you send a Fish?

A post-cod.

Dear Patrick,
Having a great time.
Wish you were here!
Oh, yeah! You are!
Love,
Spongebob

Patrick Star
Under a Rock
Bikini Bottom

What do you call a lobster
that won't share?

Shellfish!

Here Are the Answers—
Water the
questions?

(In these riddles
the answer
comes first!)

A cream Puff.

What do you get when you
cross SpongeBob's boating
instructor with a pastry?

The Grape Barrier Reef.

What's purple and lies
near Australia?

AUSTRALIA

"Kelp! Kelp!"

What do you say when you're attacked by seaweed?

The head conch-o.

What do you call a mollusk boss?

Briny Rhymes

What do you call? . . .

Gary's beach bucket?
A snail pail.

a talkative sandwich?
A chatty patty.

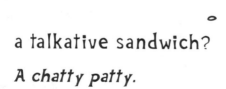

a country of crabs?
A crustacean nation.

letters to Pearl?
Whale mail.

damp sleepwear?

Clammy jammies.

a gangster shellfish?

A mobster lobster.

a shellfish taxi?

A crab cab.

a traffic tie-up by the shore?

A clam jam.

Nautical Knock-Knocks

Knock-knock.
Who's there?
Porpoise.
Porpoise who?
Porpoise of my
visit is to tell
knock-knocks!

Knock-knock.
Who's there?
Whale.
Whale who?
Whale you open the door
and let us in?

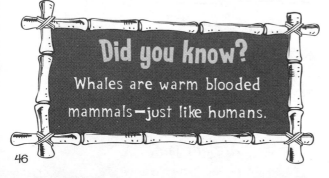

Did you know?
Whales are warm blooded
mammals—just like humans.

Knock-knock.
Who's there?
Foam.
Foam who?
Foam call—it's for you!

Knock-knock.
Who's there?
Smelda.
Smelda who?
Smelda dead fish—pee-yew!

Knock-knock.
Who's there?
Seashore.
Seashore
who?
Seashore
wants you
to tell another
knock-knock joke!

Knock-knock.
Who's there?
Swimwear.
Swimwear who?
Swimwear jellyfish
won't find you!

Knock-knock.
Who's there?
Water.
Water who?
Water you doing inside
on a sunny day?

Knock-knock.
Who's there?
Herring.
Herring who?
Herring some awful
knock-knock jokes!